P9-DWD-687

SLUGGER

by Susan Pearson

illustrated by David Slonim

AMAZON CHILDREN'S PUBLISHING

Amazon Publishing
Attn: Amazon Children's Publishing
P.O. Box 400818
Las Vegas, NV 89140
www.amazon.com/amazonchildrenspublishing

Library of Congress Cataloging-in-Publication Data available upon request.

9781477816417 (hardcover)
9781477866412 (eBook)

The illustrations were rendered in acrylic, pencil and ball point pen on illustration board.
Book design by Katrina Damkœhler
Editor: Margery Cuyler

Printed in China (R)
First edition
10 9 8 7 6 5 4 3 2 1

For Sakai and Matthias—S. P.

To Robert—D. S.

Ollie was a slug who loved baseball. He loved the teams—especially the Creepy Crawlers. He loved the crack of the bat and the roar of the crowd.

Most of all, he loved the players. Grasshopper Bob. Bombardier Bill. Mickey Mantis. Babe Beetle.

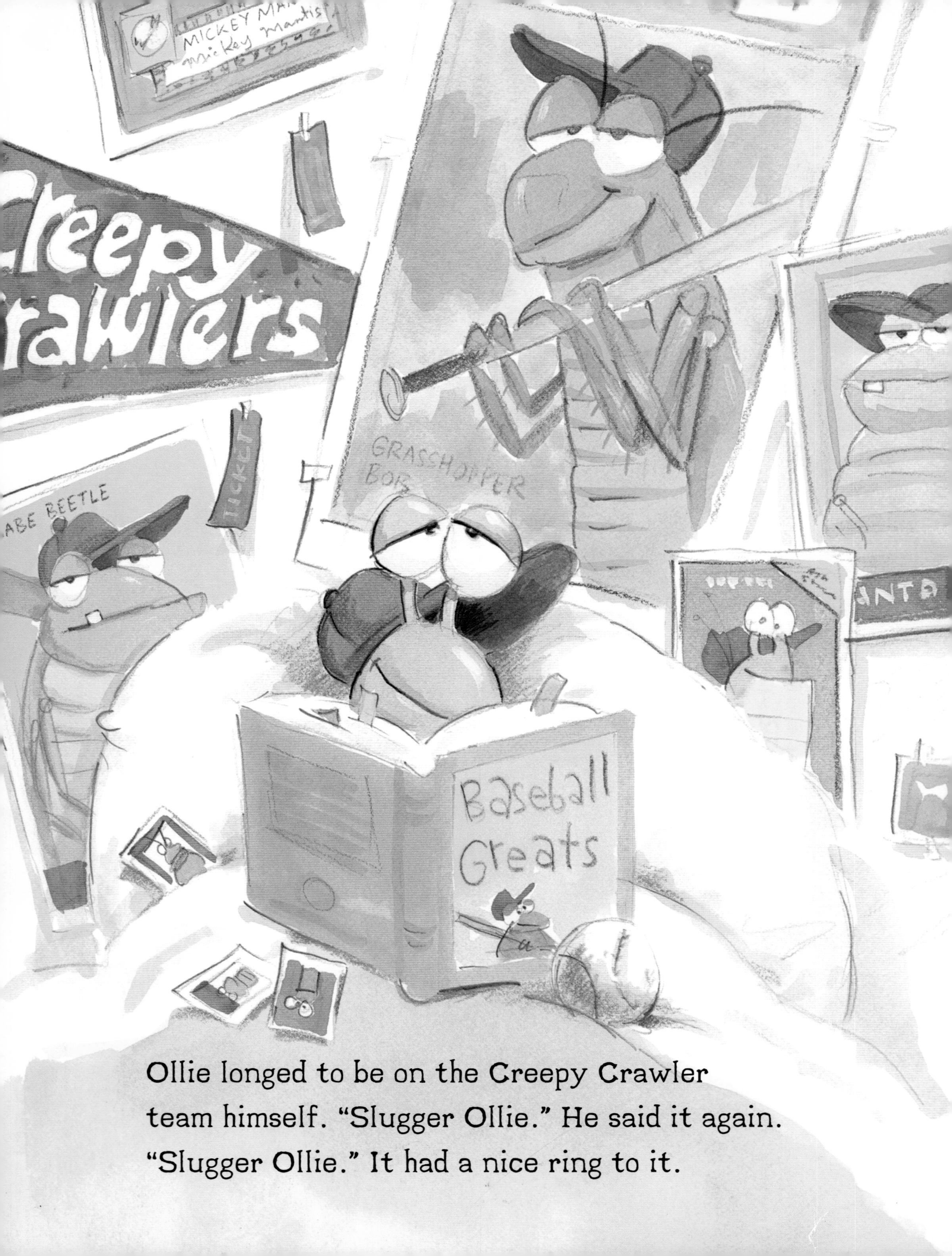

Ollie longed to be on the Creepy Crawler team himself. "Slugger Ollie." He said it again. "Slugger Ollie." It had a nice ring to it.

True, he wasn't much of a pitcher.

He wasn't much of a catcher, either.

And he was pretty slow at running the bases.

His only hope was as a slugger.

"Are you crazy?" shouted Lenny Leafhopper.

"You can't even hold a bat!" shouted Locust Lou.

This was true, but Ollie was one determined slug.

Ollie got his friend Sammy Stinkbug to pitch for him.

Then he put on his SUPER-SLUGGER-HARD-HEAD-#12 helmet and stepped up to the plate.

At first, Ollie had a little trouble connecting. Sammy's screwballs flew right past him.

Curveballs made him dizzy.

Fastballs made him want to duck.

But Ollie was a slug with a dream.
Day after day, in wind . . .

and rain . . .

and sweltering sun,
he kept at it.

Can we quit now?
Just one more! Sock it to me!!

Whack!

It was a hit at last! And it was going . . .
going . . . GONE! You coulda hung that baby
on a star. It woulda been a home run for sure—
if anyone had seen it.

Ollie went off to find Coach Roach.

"I've practiced and practiced," said Ollie. "And I'm hitting pretty strong. Can I join the team now?"

Ollie had to do a lot of talking, but finally Coach Roach agreed. "Okay. I'll let you play in the Swingin' Stinger game tonight," he said. "But don't blow it, kid. This is your only chance to make the team."

The game was tied at the bottom of the ninth, and the Creepy Crawlers had two outs, when it started to rain.

Whizzer Wasp was on the mound for the Swingin' Stingers, and Grasshopper Bob was up to bat.

Grasshopper hit a ground ball to left field and skidded over the slippery mud to first. SAFE!

Babe Beetle hit a line drive into right field, where it landed in a big puddle. SPLASH! The Swingin' Stinger fielders were a muddy mess, and Babe was SAFE!

Then Locust Lou hit another grounder. He tripped in the muck on his way to first—but he made it. The bases were loaded. And then . . .

Ollie was up to bat.

He looked out through the rain—at Locust on first, and Babe on second, and Grasshopper Bob on third.

Ollie shivered. It was up to him to drive Grasshopper home for the winning run.

Whizzer wound up and delivered a curveball.
Ollie felt dizzy.
STRIKE
ONE!

Then a screwball over the plate flew right past him.

"Hey batta batta!" The Swingin' Stinger fans were screaming.

Ollie thought about the next pitch. He needed to try something new, something no one would be expecting.

And then the fastball was on its way. . . .

Ollie didn't duck. He held his head low. He took aim. And BAM! The ball went speeding along the wet grass, right between Whizzer's legs.

Ollie took off for first. He may not have been the fastest Creepy Crawler on the field, but mud is a slug's dream come true.

The Stingers slipped and lurched all over the mud-slicked field trying to get hold of the ball . . .

. . . while Ollie slid happily along to first base and Grasshopper Bob leapt home for the winning run!

The Creepy Crawlers went wild. The Swingin' Stingers slunk off the field as the fans rushed on. What a hit! What a game! What a night!

"Ya did it, Slugger," said Coach Roach. "You're on the team."

It was a **SLUGGIFEROUS DAY!**—
for Slugger Ollie . . .

. . . and for all the little sluggers
with big dreams of their own!